The Season to Be Jolly
10 heartwarming and humorous short stories for Christmas and the festive season

Stefania Hartley

THE SICILIAN MAMA

ALSO AVAILABLE AS
EBOOK AND LARGE PRINT

Copyright © 2025 Stefania
Hartley

ISBN: 978-1-914606-66-3

These short stories were first
published individually in The
People's Friend magazine.

Edited by Sandy Salisbury
Cover by Joseph Witchall
https://josephwitchall.com/

To Bernadette Venezia

CONTENTS

1. ONE STEP CLOSER

Rosella's flight was running so late that it would be almost Christmas when she landed. She was really looking forward to spending the special day with her daughter, granddaughter and son-in-law.

Other than on video calls, she hadn't seen them for so long! How tall would little Sara be now?

Under the seat in front of her Rosella slipped her feet out of her shiny new red patent leather flats and smiled. She had fallen in love with these shoes as soon as she'd seen them in the shop window and couldn't resist buying them. But maybe they were more appropriate for a child than a grandmother. What was her daughter going to say about them? One thing was certain—Giada would notice them.

The captain announced that they were about to land at Bristol Airport.

Rosella's heart revved up in sync with the

engines and not just out of excitement. She was afraid of flying.

The aircraft rattled through a cloud bank and Rosella gripped her armrests. Even if it was a long way from Catania to Bristol, next time she would look into coming by train. It would be better for the environment, too.

Finally the aeroplane's wheels touched down. Rosella was about to clap for the pilot, but noticed that no one else was and she stopped just in time. Instead, she wriggled back into her faux-fur coat, put on her hat and gloves and got ready to disembark.

As she stepped out of the plane and onto the stairs with all that fur on, she realised that England wasn't quite Lapland. By the time she got to the luggage collection belt she was too warm, and when she finally dragged her suitcases out of the arrivals gate she was actually sweating.

"You're only missing a pair of skis," her daughter said with a smile, hugging her.

"I know. I've overdone it."

"But I love your red shoes."

Rosella grinned. It was funny how she was just as keen to impress her daughter as she had been to impress her own mother in her younger years.

"I'm sorry that you've had to come and

collect me so late," she said.

"It's no problem. Andy is putting Sara to bed. We haven't told her that you are coming, just in case the flight was cancelled or delayed. If she'd known, she would have refused to go to sleep. You'll be her Christmas surprise," Giada said, smiling.

What a lovely thing to be! She just hoped that she would not to be a Christmas disappointment.

***

It was almost midnight when Rosella and Giada finally got home.

"Are you hungry? I can warm you up some soup," Giada offered.

Rosella had had nothing to eat since the morning, but she still wasn't hungry. The nerves of flying had knotted her stomach.

"No, thanks, I'm fine."

Seeing Giada leave her shoes by the door, Rosella removed hers too.

She had just checked her tights for holes in the toes when her son-in-law appeared and welcomed her with a hug and a kiss.

"It's nice of you to come. What a great Christmas present for Sara!" he exclaimed in English mixed with Italian, and she felt warm inside, even as he took her coat off her shoulders.

Knowing that Sara would surely give them all an early start the next day, they said goodnight to each other shortly after. Then Rosella pulled her presents out of her suitcase and tiptoed downstairs to put them under the Christmas tree. Finally she changed into her nightie and slipped gratefully into bed.

As soon as she lay down and started to relax, her stomach grumbled. Rosella turned on the other side and tried to ignore it, but it kept on rumbling.

She couldn't help thinking about the soup Giada had offered her. Creamy tomato was her favourite, but she also loved pumpkin, carrot and coriander, and pea and mint—especially if it came with a hint of smoked bacon…

Oh, dear, she was never going to sleep like this! She had to sneak down to the kitchen and get something to eat.

Rosella slipped out of bed, gingerly opened her door and climbed down the stair as quietly as she could.

Just as Giada had promised, there was a bowl of soup in the fridge. It was tomato soup, too! But how was she going to warm it up without making a noise?

To use the hob she would have to pull a pot out of the cupboard, which is never a silent activity. The microwave was going to whirr and ping.

No. She would have to eat it cold.

She put the cold bowl down on the table, ever so carefully took a spoon out of the cutlery drawer and sat down to eat.

She was so hungry that, even cold, it was delicious. But she was only halfway through the bowl when she started shivering.

She was only in her nightie and the cold soup was chilling her from the inside out. She thought about fetching her dressing gown from her room, but that would mean stepping on the creaky floorboard on the stairs twice more. Was there anything else she could put on without going upstairs? Oh, yes—her fur coat!

***

Sara woke up in a sweat. She had dreamed that Father Christmas had come but hadn't found any biscuits or milk, so he had left sad and hungry.

Last night, before going to bed, she and Daddy had forgotten to prepare the treats for him. Had Father Christmas already come to their house or was that just a dream?

She jumped out of bed and ran to the window. It was still dark outside, so maybe she wasn't too late.

She opened her bedroom door very slowly—she must not wake Mum and Dad or scare off Father Christmas. She slipped through the gap and tiptoed down the stairs.

At the bottom of the stairs, she saw a pair of shiny red shoes by the front door and gasped. They were the same colour as Father Christmas's clothes!

They were ladies' shoes, so maybe Father Christmas had sent Mother Christmas instead.

A beautiful white faux-fur hat lay on top of the shoe cabinet next to some gloves. They had to be Mother Christmas's, too. And if her shoes, hat and gloves were by the front door, she must still be in the house!

Sara knew that she had to prepare a cup of milk and a plate of biscuits quickly.

As she crept past the sitting room, she couldn't help slowing down and peeking in. Three new parcels sat under the Christmas tree. They hadn't been there before she'd gone to bed.

She grinned.

Then her gaze fell on a heap of brown fur lying curled up on the sofa. Was that a reindeer? Sara had to cover her mouth with both her hands to stop herself from squealing in excitement.

She would have liked to touch the reindeer, but didn't want to wake it up. Tonight must be very tiring for them.

But where was Mother Christmas? Sara looked around the room. Oh, no, maybe she was in the kitchen, looking for her biscuits and milk.

Sara ran to the kitchen on her tiptoes. A half-eaten bowl of soup and a licked spoon lay on the kitchen table. Mother Christmas must have found no biscuits and helped herself to the soup, but she hadn't liked it and had left it.

Sara reached up for the biscuit tin, but it was too high up on the top shelf. She pushed a chair to the counter and climbed onto it.

Balancing and jiggling, she got the tin down and put her favourite biscuits on a plate. Now the milk.

Sara opened the fridge and saw a bunch of carrots. In the book Daddy had read to her at bedtime, the reindeers loved carrots. She must give a carrot to the reindeer!

Forgetting about the milk, she picked one carrot and rushed back to the sitting room. The reindeer wasn't on the sofa anymore.

Sara rushed to the entrance hall to find that Mother Christmas's shoes were gone, too. She had left and Sara hadn't managed to see her! She ran to the sitting room window and looked out.

Mother Christmas's sleigh wasn't on the street, nor in the sky. A knot formed in Sara's throat and her chin trembled.

If she had known, she wouldn't have bothered with the biscuits but would have stayed in the sitting room and stroked the reindeer. Then, at least, she would have met Mother Christmas.

***

Rosella had no idea where Andy had put her coat when he took it. She had looked in the entrance hall, but it wasn't hanging there. She had searched in the dining room, but it wasn't there either.

She had eventually found it on the sitting room sofa. Putting it on, she immediately felt better, only to realise that her feet were cold. The kitchen's stone floor had chilled her toes. Surely Giada wouldn't mind if she wore her shoes in the kitchen just this once.

She noticed her hat on top of the shoe cabinet. She might as well put that on too.

With her hat, coat and shoes on, she crept back to the kitchen, ready to attack the rest of the soup.

But on the kitchen table, next to the bowl of soup, there was now a plate of biscuits.

It surely hadn't been there before.

"Mother Christmas!" a child called behind her.

Rosella's poor English was enough to work

out who her granddaughter had mistaken her for. Now the biscuits left on the table made sense.

Rosella turned slowly, cringing at the thought of the disappointment she was about to see on her granddaughter's face.

"*Ciao, amore mio*—hello, my love. I'm sorry, it's only me, your nonna."

But what Rosella saw on Sara's face wasn't disappointment. A frown of confusion turned into open-mouthed surprise, and finally a big grin spread across her sweet little face.

"Nonna!" Sara cried out, running into Rosella's arms. "You're not Mother Christmas!" the child exclaimed after the tightest hug and a shower of kisses.

"I'm sorry, no."

"And this isn't a reindeer," Sara said, stroking the soft faux-fur of Rosella's coat.

"I'm afraid not. I've come from the sky, yes, but not on a sleigh pulled by reindeer. I'm not Mother Christmas."

"You mustn't be sorry. I prefer you a million times," Sara told her.

"Thank you, *amore*," Rosella murmured, touched. "I'm really happy to see you too."

Sara looked down at Rosella's feet. "You've got Christmas shoes, so you can be Grandmother Christmas, if you want."

"Do you like my shoes?" Rosella asked.

"I love them!"

Rosella smiled. Under the Christmas tree, there was one pair for Giada and another for Sara.

2. MANY HANDS

Christmas was coming sooner every year, Melina thought with dismay when the butcher informed her that he was taking Christmas bookings.

She still hadn't recovered from last year's effort. But as soon as she got home, she sat down with pen and paper and started planning her family's Christmas lunch.

For a starter, she could make Tanino's favourite Sicilian *sfincione* pizza. A pasta bake with minced beef and mortadella ham would do nicely for the first course. For the second, Melina was torn between her granddaughter's favourite *falsomagro* beef roulade, or the sardine rolls with breadcrumbs, pine nuts and raisins, which her daughter, Rosanna, loved.

Unable to choose, she put down both and made a note to order the sardines from the fishmonger. On the list also went her son-in-law's favourite salad—orange, fennel and olives. A green salad would go down well too, and some roasted potatoes to accompany the second course. All three side dishes went on the menu. For dessert, Tanino would buy a shortcrust pastry and dried fruit *buccellato* ring from the cake shop.

Melina reviewed her list. It was long, with many laborious, time-consuming dishes to be prepared. She was going to struggle, but she didn't want to take anything off the list. Her culinary skills were her pride and joy, and she glowed when her cooking was appreciated.

She picked up the phone and rang the butcher.

***

Tanino was surprised to find only a ball of mozzarella and two slices of bread on the table for his supper. Melina loved to cook. She must have been very busy that day.

"What have you been up to today?" he asked.

She sighed. "You won't believe it. I've had to put in our Christmas orders with the butcher! It's ridiculous how Christmas is starting earlier every year!"

Tanino stopped with his fork halfway to his mouth. "Hasn't Rosanna spoken to you yet?"

"What about?" Melina asked with a frown.

After how stressful last year's Christmas had

been for Melina, Rosanna had suggested to Tanino that she, her husband and her daughter could spend Christmas at her in-laws. It would make the other grandparents happy and give Melina a well-deserved break.

Tanino thought it was a good idea but wondered how Melina would take it. Clearly neither he nor Rosanna had been brave enough to find out, each hoping that the other would tell Melina first.

Now Melina had put in her Christmas orders. Tanino had to tell her.

"Rosanna and family are, er…thinking of spending Christmas with the other grandparents," he said, avoiding her gaze.

"What? Nobody told me! They can't change the plan at the last minute like this!"

"You've just said that it was too early to plan Christmas," Tanino replied.

"And what about us? Are we to spend Christmas on our own?" Melina asked.

"Why not?" Tanino said.

Tanino usually spent Christmas collecting orders from butchers and cake shops, lengthening tables, carrying chairs and serving drinks. But by far the worst part was having a frantic, tired wife.

"We could have a quiet Christmas, just you and me. No need to cook up a feast. We can just enjoy each other's company."

"We can do that any day!" Melina said, throwing her hands in the air. "I want to spend Christmas with my daughter and my granddaughter!"

"They live downstairs—we see them every day," Tanino pointed out. "It's only right that, once in a while, they spend Christmas with the other grandparents too."

**

"I hadn't told you yet because I was waiting for an answer from Alida and Stefano," Rosanna said when Melina confronted her.

"So it was you who asked to spend Christmas with them?"

Melina was shocked. The betrayal was worse than she had imagined.

A horrible thought crossed her mind. Maybe the other grandma, Alida, was a better cook than her.

"No, Mamma. I actually asked them if you and Papà could come too. As luck would have it, Alida and Stefano have just replied." Rosanna grinned. "They'd be delighted to have you."

Panic swamped Melina. "We can't go!"

"Why not? It would be lovely, and you wouldn't have to lift a finger," Tanino put in.

But Melina enjoyed lifting fingers—and

arms, too. Since she was a little girl, Melina had always spent Christmas in the kitchen, first helping in her grandma's kitchen, then in her mum's, then cooking in her own. Yes, sometimes the work was a bit much, but if she didn't cook at Christmas, what else would she do?

"I don't mind working in the kitchen," Melina said candidly.

Rosanna smiled. "I know. That's why you never let me help you. But for once, you can be a guest."

Melina had no idea how to be a guest. She had always been the host at Christmas.

"It would make Valentina very happy to have all her grandparents with her at Christmas," Rosanna said. "Please, Mamma, do it for her."

Melina wasn't able to deny her granddaughter anything.

"Fine. We'll go."

***

As soon as Melina stepped through the door of Alida and Stefano's flat, she offered to help in the kitchen.

"It's all under control," Alida said with a big smile.

When the meal started, Melina found that Alida had good reasons to smile. Starters, firsts, mains and sides—every dish was delicious and prepared to the highest standard.

In comparison, Melina felt like a rookie in the kitchen, and a terrible host, too. Unlike her, Alida was relaxed, attentive and available for conversation. Melina felt smaller with every mouthful.

Just after dessert, Melina excused herself and made her way down the corridor to the bathroom, but she had forgotten where it was.

She opened the first door and found herself in the kitchen instead.

Melina looked around and gasped.

Every surface was littered with aluminium trays, paper bags and cardboard boxes bearing the name of a catering company.

All those wonderful dishes had looked professional—because they were!

Melina's inferiority complex crumbled, and jealousy was replaced by rising sympathy. Poor Alida. She must be a terrible cook to have resorted to caterers!

This explained why she had refused Melina's offer of help—she had a secret to protect.

Ignited by grandmotherly solidarity, Melina decided to do all she could to prevent anyone else discovering Alida's embarrassing secret.

First, all those trays and boxes must disappear.

Melina emptied the leftovers into Alida's own crockery then squashed boxes and trays into the bin, pushing them as far down as they would go.

"Mum, are you all right?" Rosanna called from the corridor.

Oh, no. Melina's absence from the table had been noticed.

She still had a few boxes left, but couldn't risk Rosanna coming into the kitchen.

"All fine," Melina said, shooting out of the kitchen and closing the door behind her. "I was just getting some water."

***

Melina returned to the dining room just as Alida got up to clear the table.

"Let us help you," Tanino said, getting up too.

"No!" Melina stopped him with her hand.

Alida disappeared into the corridor.

Stefano chuckled. "Don't worry, Melina. In our household men are allowed to help, too."

"Yes. In fact, we're all going to help. Many hands make lighter work," Rosanna said, standing up.

No! Everyone was standing up to take their plates to the kitchen!

Melina leapt up from her chair and stood in their way, blocking the entry to the corridor.

"I'm sure Alida doesn't appreciate, er, interference in her kitchen," Melina said.

If she couldn't stop them going to the kitchen, she must at least delay them long enough for Alida to clear away the last boxes.

"She's fine about it, Mum," Rosanna said. "Alida isn't jealous of her kitchen. Now, let us through, please."

"Alida? Can we come into the kitchen?" Melina called down the corridor.

"One moment, please," Alida replied.

"My arms are tired. These plates are heavy," Valentina complained.

"I'm sorry, sweetheart, but your other grandma has told us to wait," Melina said without budging.

***

"What were you asking, Melina? I couldn't hear," Alida said, emerging from the kitchen with a smile. She took in the scene and frowned. "What's the matter?"

Everyone answered at once, but Alida turned to Melina.

"I asked everyone to wait for your permission to enter the kitchen," Melina explained with a wink.

"It's absolutely fine. You can all go in," Alida said with a smile. "I couldn't hear you because I was sorting the caterers' packaging into our recycling bags. Someone had stuffed everything in the undifferentiated waste bin so I had to dig inside and pull it all out."

Melina froze. Why had Alida told her secret?

***

When the table had been cleared and the others were setting up the bingo, Melina found herself alone in the kitchen with Alida.

It was her chance to ask the question.

"Do you not mind people knowing that you've used caterers?"

"Not at all," Alida said good-naturedly. "Christmas isn't a cooking competition. It's about spending time with family and friends. If I had cooked this meal, I would have been exhausted and I would have spent all my time in the kitchen instead of with you all."

"You are right. I should take a leaf out of your book," Melina confessed. "Every Christmas, I run myself into the ground and become grumpy and insufferable to be around."

"Family is more important than food," Alida declared solemnly.

The coffee was gurgling inside the percolator. Alida turned off the flame and Melina placed the percolator on the serving tray.

"Wait. Don't take it to the sitting room yet.

I've made some biscuits to go with it," Alida said, pulling a tray of beautiful pistachio and lemon biscuits out of the oven.

Melina complimented them and Alida looked very pleased.

They walked to the sitting room, Alida in front with the biscuits, and Melina behind with the coffee.

But as they got to the sitting room, nobody paid them any attention. Everyone was crowding around a box of chocolate biscuits which Michele was passing around.

Alida's face contorted in displeasure. "Stop that! We're having my biscuits now!" she snapped at her son.

Melina patted her arm to calm her down. "Family before food, Alida, remember?"

3. MIDNIGHT MEETING

"We should have left earlier. Now all the seats have been taken," his mother complained, surveying the church.

"There are plenty of seats left," Riccardo said in a conciliatory tone.

"But not our usual seats. You don't care because you always give up your seat anyway," she said grouchily.

His mother was always in a bad mood on Christmas Eve. The midnight Mass was past her bedtime, and she had spent the day on her feet, arranging the church flowers.

"I don't understand why these people only come to church at Christmas," she ranted as they made their way to the front. "If they can't be bothered to come every week, they shouldn't come at all."

"They might be visitors, come to spend Christmas with family," Riccardo replied.

"And they even have the cheek to bring

children along at this time of night!"

If any church celebration was meant for children, it was Christmas, Riccardo thought.

"Mamma, sit here," he said, having found an empty seat at the end of a pew.

A man smiled at them and shuffled over to make space.

"And you?"

He smiled at her. "I'll stand, of course."

***

Giorgia sat down and looked at the stranger who had shuffled over on the pew to make space for her. She had never seen him before, so he must be one of the Christmas crowd.

Giorgia had stopped enjoying Christmas some time ago. Year after year, she had asked God for a simple Christmas gift—something that everyone else seemed to have in abundance. Grandchildren.

But her only son, Riccardo, was now thirty-six and still uninterested in starting a family.

Coming to church at Christmas and seeing happy grandparents fill the pews with their children and grandchildren only reminded her of how little God liked her.

The bells rang, the guitars strummed, and the youth choir stood up and started singing a cheerful song about Jesus being born today. Giorgia pulled herself up to standing and sighed softly.

***

Riccardo loved the Christmas crowd. As well as strangers, it included old classmates and childhood friends—people who had left Palermo to study or work and were spending the festivities with family.

He particularly wished to see one of them. Ilaria.

She'd been his first love when they were teenagers, but she had broken up with him when she left to study in Milan.

Mutual friends had then told him that she had got a job there and was settled, but nobody could tell him if she had a husband and a family of her own.

It was better this way. He would rather not know.

A couple of times he had caught glimpses of her at Christmas midnight Mass, but had never plucked up the courage to speak to her, and she had never come to him.

From the back of the church, a child carrying a terracotta Baby Jesus led the procession, followed by the priest and the altar servers.

She must have been about six years old and clutched the baby tightly to her chest. She navigated the step at the front of the church successfully, then stopped.

The manger where she was meant to lay the baby was too far for her arms, unless she stepped over the cordon of ivy and moss and into the nativity scene.

The priest and the altar servers couldn't see the little girl's panicked eyes from where they were standing, but Riccardo could.

He was about to rush to the girl's help when a woman—possibly her mother—hurried to the front. With a smile, she took Baby Jesus from the girl's hands and, stretching over, gently laid him down in the manger.

Riccardo's heart swelled with relief, but it lasted only a second. When mother and daughter returned to the pews, he saw that the girl's mother was Ilaria.

The hope he had secretly held all these years shattered like a glass bauble on the floor.

Ilaria had a family of her own, and she would never return to him.

***

When they sat down in their pew, Ilaria hugged Nina.

"You've done really well," she whispered.

Nina hugged her back and Ilaria's heart melted a little.

The social worker had warned her that she would get attached to her foster child. Giving

Nina back was going to be hard, but give her back she must, as soon as a couple came forward to adopt her. If only she could adopt her herself… But Italian law didn't look favourably on single adopters.

Ilaria tried to concentrate on the service, but her mind kept flitting away. This was the church where she had grown up, and memories of her youth and the choices she had made flooded her mind.

Putting her studies and career above everything had got her an engineering job she loved, but she had missed out on a man's love and a family of her own.

Breaking up with Riccardo when they were eighteen had been the biggest sacrifice she'd made for her career. She had broken his heart, and her own heart too.

Was he here tonight?

She'd caught glimpses of him at past Christmas Masses, but she had never dared go over and say hello. She felt too guilty about the hurt she'd caused him.

Nina pulled her hand and brought her back from her reverie.

"Yes, sweetie?"

"I need the toilet."

***

The thought of Ilaria in a relationship with

another man made Riccardo feel physically unwell. He could do with splashing some cold water on his face.

He told his mother he was going to the toilet and took the side door to the sacristy. He walked down the quiet corridor, turned the corner, and found someone already waiting at the toilets.

Ilaria was standing outside the Ladies', talking to someone through the door. Possibly her child.

Riccardo hadn't been this close to her since the day they had parted, and she looked even more beautiful than he remembered.

He swallowed hard. A splash of cold water on his face wouldn't cut it now. He had to go away before he made a fool of himself.

He turned to leave, but a voice stopped him.

"Hi, Riccardo."

He turned slowly to give himself time to rearrange his face into a convincingly surprised smile.

"Oh, hi, Ilaria."

***

Ilaria was sure that he had seen her but would have gone away if she hadn't called him. In fact, she had a feeling that he was going away *because* he had seen her.

Fair enough. She had hurt him a lot.

Back when they were eighteen, he'd told her that he'd wait for her, but she hadn't given him the chance.

She hadn't wanted anything holding her back, so she had cut the strings of their relationship. She hadn't realised, though, that she was cutting the strings of her own heart.

It had taken her a long time to heal, and if the pain he had been through was anything like hers, he had every right to avoid her.

She shouldn't have stopped him leaving the room, especially because, now that she had, she didn't know what to say.

Nina broke the silence.

"I've finished, but I can't get out," she announced from inside the toilet.

Ilaria pushed down on the door handle, but the door didn't budge.

"Have you locked the door?" she asked Nina.

"Yes," the girl answered guiltily.

Ilaria had assured her there was no need to lock herself in because she'd be guarding the door.

She sighed. Being on the wrong side of the door, she was powerless to set Nina free, and she had to rely on her to help herself.

"Turn the lock the other way," Ilaria suggested through the door.

"Which way?"

"Try one way, then the other."

There was some clunking.

"I can't!" Nina said, then burst into sobs.

Nina wasn't going to respond to instructions if she was in the throes of a meltdown!

"I'll try to get in through the window," Riccardo said. "Warn her so she doesn't get scared."

Before Ilaria could thank him, he was off.

***

Thankfully the window of the ladies' toilet was open.

"Hello," Riccardo called through the gap.

The girl stopped crying.

"Are you the prince who's come to rescue me?" she asked.

"Yes."

He couldn't help wondering if it been Ilaria who imagined him as a prince, or the girl.

The gap in the window was wide enough for him to stick his arm through, unhook the latch and open the window fully. He lifted himself up and popped his head in.

"Hello," Nina said.

"Hello. May I come in?"

She smiled. "Yes."

With some difficulty, he clambered through the window and was inside. The door lock was faulty and, for a moment, he wondered if he might have to take Nina out through the window.

With a little patience, he eventually managed to open the door and found himself face-to-face with Ilaria. A beautiful smile lit up her face and Riccardo's heart did a somersault.

"Thank you!" she told him.

For a dizzying moment, he thought that she might be about to hug him, but she hugged her girl instead.

"Has your daughter finished?" a woman asked from the queue that had formed for the toilet.

"I think so, but she's not my daughter," Riccardo replied.

The woman scowled.

"Yes, we're done," Ilaria said, then turned to Riccardo. "Are you going back to the service?"

"Yes."

They walked down the corridor side by side, with the little girl skipping a few paces in front of them.

"That woman gave you such a look," Ilaria whispered to him. "But Nina is not my daughter either."

"Oh? Who is she, then?"

A ray of hope filtered through the clouds of Riccardo's heart.

"I'm her foster parent. I'd love to adopt her, but I'm single," she said sadly.

Riccardo almost tripped over his own feet. Ilaria didn't have another man.

***

Giorgia kept looking at the door to the sacristy. Why wasn't her son back yet?

Finally the door to the sacristy opened, and there was Riccardo with a woman and a child. Riccardo looked radiant, and the three of them looked like a happy family.

Giorgia's heart leapt in her chest. This was where she had been going wrong all these years! She had asked for grandchildren when she should have first asked for a wife for her son instead!

***

"Who was that woman you were talking to?" Giorgia asked her son when they walked back to the car.

"Who?" he said with unconvincing nonchalance.

"The one you swapped phones numbers with."

"An old friend," he said, but he couldn't hide the glow on his face or the spring in his step.

There was definitely something between them.

Giorgia hid a smile too. "Good. We always like to see the Christmas crowd."

4. ALL YOU CAN EAT

I know when Christmas is near because the postman comes to our house every day. Most of the parcels are for me or my brother, but sometimes they're for Mum and Dad, or for the whole family. Like this morning.

"Can I open it?" I asked Dad, but Geronimo, my little brother, said it wasn't fair because he wanted to open it too.

So Dad said that Mum would open it when she got home, because the parcel was from Italy and it must be from her family.

Geronimo and I climbed on the sofa and waited at the window. Both of us wanted to be the first to see Mum and tell her about the parcel from Italy.

But when we ran to the door and shouted at the same time, Mum told us she couldn't understand anything we were saying.

"There's a parcel from Italy and everyone is waiting for you to open it," Dad said, and passed her the parcel.

"Can it wait until I've washed my hands?" she asked.

"No!" Geronimo and I cried at the same time.

We agree sometimes.

We all went to the sitting room and Mum put the parcel on the floor and checked the writing on it. "I wonder who it's from."

"Open it!" Geronimo and I chorused.

Dad took a knife from the kitchen and gave it to Mum. She cut the tape and opened the box. Inside, there was a red and golden tin that said *Panettone di Milano*.

"What's that, Mum?" Geronimo asked, because he's small and doesn't know many things.

"It's a cake that people in Italy eat for Christmas," I told him.

"Who is it from?" Dad asked.

"There's no card inside," Mum replied.

"Here's a card!" I exclaimed.

"That's only the shop's business card," Dad said.

We checked the outside of the box but there was only the name of the shop.

"It's very nice of the shop to send us a present," Geronimo remarked.

"Let's check the Customs declaration

form," Mum suggested, pulling a sheet out of a plastic pocket that was stuck on the box.

"What does it say?" I asked.

"It's no use," Mum said, shaking her head. "It's been filled in by the shop."

"How do the shop people know us?" Geronimo asked.

"Can we still eat it?" I asked.

"I know who sent it!" Geronimo cried, jumping up.

"Who?" Mum asked.

"Father Christmas, of course!"

Unfortunately Mum said that we couldn't eat the *panettone* before Christmas. I soon wished we hadn't received the parcel because, from the moment we opened it, I wanted to eat that panettone.

Also, Mum had been in a bad mood ever since. Maybe she didn't like panettone.

"How are we going to thank the people who sent it to us, let alone send them a present, if we don't know who they are?" Mum kept saying.

"It's got to be your brother. He lives in Milan," Dad told her.

"But we stopped giving each other Christmas presents ages ago. We barely speak to each other these days."

"Have you had a fight?" I asked Mum.

"No."

"Your mother doesn't get on with her brother's wife," Dad whispered in my ear.

"If I have to start sending presents to people in Italy too, I don't know where I'm going to find the money or the time!" Mum grumbled, walking around the house, picking things up and putting them back in the same places.

When Mum does that, I keep away, but Dad doesn't understand that he should keep away too.

"Maybe your brother has had a promotion or something else he wanted to celebrate. Didn't you say that people in Italy receive a thirteenth month's salary in December to help them with Christmas shopping?"

"Yes."

"You'll have to call him and ask him if he sent us the panettone."

Mum groaned.

***

When Mum called Uncle Mario, I played with my Lego near her so that I could listen.

She asked Uncle Mario about his job, his children and the weather in Milan, but she didn't ask about the panettone for ages.

I was so worried that she was going to forget it that I thought I should climb on a chair to get the panettone down from the shelf and bring it to her to remind her.

"By the way, did you send us a panettone?" she asked finally.

I don't know what Uncle Mario said, but Mum said, "No, don't worry. I wasn't expecting you to send anything. It's just that it came from a shop in Milan and I don't know anyone else in Milan. No, really, I wasn't expecting you to..."

When Mum finished the call, her cheeks and her ears were red.

"It wasn't my brother," she told Dad.

"So who was it?" Dad asked.

"I don't know, but I'm not going to make any more calls like that."

Despite what she said, Mum called her cousin in Rome, her friend in Venice and my aunt in Palermo. None of them sent the panettone, so the mystery continued.

***

Uncle John called us a few days later, and I answered the phone.

"Have you received my parcel? The website says it's been delivered," he said.

"No. We've only received a parcel from Italy," I replied.

"That's the one! So you got the panettone."

"But it's from Milan and you're in England, Uncle John," I pointed out.

"I bought it online. I thought your family might like a panettone from the city that invented them," he explained.

"Thank you!"

"I hope you enjoy it."

"I don't think Mum will, but she will be very happy to know who sent it. We've tried for three days to work it out."

I was happy too, because I never thought I would be the one to solve the mystery.

***

Another parcel arrived a few days later. It had Mum's name on, so Geronimo and I couldn't open it, but that was okay by me, so long as Geronimo wasn't allowed to open it either.

"It comes from France. It must be from the Fontaines," Mum guessed.

The Fontaines are our French friends from the caravan camp where we go every summer.

"Oh, no. Now I have two parcels to reciprocate," Mum said.

"Don't worry, dear. People don't keep a tally of who sent them something and who didn't," Dad told her.

Mum stopped opening the parcel and looked at him. "Your sister has a notebook for that exact thing."

She opened the box and pulled out a metal

tin.

"Christmas butter biscuits. I love them!" Mum cried.

"Can we try them?" I asked.

"Not before Christmas."

Mum pulled out her phone, took a picture of Geronimo and me holding the tin, and sent it to the Fontaines.

"The French biscuits aren't from the Fontaines," Mum told us a few minutes later, looking at her phone.

"Wasn't there a card in the parcel?" Dad asked.

"No. Just the shop's business card."

"Auntie Rachel has been on holiday to France," I reminded them.

Mum shook her head. "If Auntie Rachel had sent it, she would have addressed it to Dad, not me."

Dad frowned.

"I'll call her and we'll see who's right," he said.

But Mum was right. It hadn't been Auntie Rachel.

Now we had a new mystery: the mystery of the French biscuits.

***

Dad called a cousin who had married a French man and moved to France.

She hadn't sent the biscuits, but they had a long chat with lots of laughing.

Mum rang the shop in Paris to ask them who had ordered the biscuits for us, but they didn't understand her French and she didn't understand their English.

Mum was getting more and more stressed about it.

"It'll soon be too late to send them something in return!" she cried.

"Stop worrying about it. Just enjoy the love that other people give you," Dad replied, kissing her.

Two days later, Uncle Mario called Mum. This time, I was close enough to hear what he was saying.

"I'm sorry I confused you. Someone had already sent you a panettone from Milan, and I remembered that you go on holiday to France every summer. I thought that some French biscuits would remind you of your holidays," Uncle Mario explained.

The mystery of the French biscuits was solved!

"I'm sorry I asked you about the panettone," Mum apologised. "I didn't mean to suggest that I was expecting to receive something from you."

"You have nothing to be sorry about. You

just gave me the idea and I liked it. This Christmas, when you eat our biscuits, it'll be as if we were there with you," he added.

***

Mum must have given the idea to all the other people she had called. Now we have a box of madeleines from the Fontaines, a pandoro Christmas cake from Mum's cousin in Rome, a *buccellato* fig cake from my aunt in Palermo, almond nougat from Mum's friend in Venice and a Yorkshire parkin from Auntie Rachel. This time there were cards in every parcel, so we had no more mysteries to solve.

"Oh, dear. I have pushed all these people to send us presents! And what are we going to do with all this food?" Mum wondered.

"Eat it!" I exclaimed.

"It's too much for us," Mum pointed out.

"I have a better idea," Dad put in.

***

"Is the food going to be enough?" Mum is asking Dad.

It was his idea to invite everyone for Christmas lunch.

"It'll be fine," Dad's saying.

Auntie Rachel, Uncle John and Uncle Mario have said yes, and everyone else has said that they'd love to see us on videocall.

Uncle Mario is flying here with his wife and

his children, who are my cousins, even if I've never met them.

Mum has promised Geronimo that he can cut the panettone, and she's promised me that I can put the icing sugar on the pandoro. It's fun to do, because you don't pour the sugar on top. You put the sugar into the bag with the cake, then you swing and shake the bag around as hard as you like, so the cake gets coated all over like a snowy white mountain.

I think this is going to be our best Christmas ever.

5. BUILDING WORKS

Silence fell on the church hall after Father's words.

"What do you mean our parish is going to be closed down?" Paul asked with a frown on behalf of everyone else at the AGM of the parish of Saint Anne.

"Our congregation has shrunk so much that keeping the parish has become unviable. The bishop has decided to incorporate this parish with Saint Gregory's. They will welcome you all with open arms."

Father would know, as he was the priest there too.

"And we'll organise car-sharing for people who can't get there."

"It all makes sense, but we're attached to our church," Julia said sadly.

"As soon as the heating is repaired, people will return," Moira added with a hopeful smile.

The church's heating system had broken

down at the start of October and attendance had plummeted as a consequence.

"I'm sorry, but the heating is not going to be repaired. The church building will be sold to a developer," Father John said.

Gasps rippled through the room.

"What will the developer do with it?" Paul asked.

"They will build houses on the car park and turn the church into a restaurant—after it's been deconsecrated, of course."

"It would make a beautiful restaurant," Moira said, looking out to the church spire and the tall stained-glass windows. "But it doesn't feel right."

"I'll be too sad to see our church turned into a restaurant. I won't be able to walk down this road ever again," Julia said, dabbing a damp eye with her monogramed handkerchief.

The following morning, Paul turned up at the presbytery's door.

"Father, the bishop cannot sell the church. Canon Law says a church building can be repurposed for 'profane but not sordid use'."

"A restaurant is not 'sordid use'," Father said.

"A restaurant could be considered a temple to gluttony."

"I don't think so, Paul. But good try."

Not long after, Julia turned up at the parish.

"Father, I've had an idea. Our church's acoustics are much better than those of the town's hall. The council should turn it into a concert hall."

"That's a great idea, Julia. But the bishop has already asked and the council hasn't the money."

***

In Sicily, the parishioners of Santa Maria, looked on in dismay at what was left of their church. The earthquake hadn't been the first to turn their church into rubble.

In fact, this version of Santa Maria hadn't been the first one. After being flattened by an earthquake in the 1970s, the original baroque church had been replaced with a modern construction.

The architects had promised it would stand until judgement day. But now concrete pillars poked out of the rubble, exposed to the shocked eyes of the townsfolk.

"At least we're all alive," one said.

Small tremors had been felt for several hours before the main quake, so everyone had had a chance to find safety.

Some of the parishioners suggested starting the rebuilding then and there with their bare hands, like Saint Francis when he rebuilt the church of Saint Damian.

Padre Giorgio told everyone to keep away until the fire brigade told them it was safe to return.

But the fire brigade never said it was safe. Instead, they cordoned off the area and put up a sign that read *DANGER*.

That year, the Christmas services were held in the school hall.

"New year, new town!" the mayor promised at the town's party, but in April there was still no sign of funds for the church's reconstruction. Nature, however, had started work on the church. Yellow wood sorrel, daisies and dandelions blossomed between bricks and pews.

***

Father John was packing the hymn books into boxes when Moira walked in with a wad of newspapers.

"You might like to use some packing material for fragile items."

"Thank you," Father said.

The only fragile item he was packing was his heart. He had to put on a brave face for his parishioners but he, too, was sad.

His gaze fell on the front page of one of the papers, which showed a photo of a town in Sicily struck by an earthquake. His heart went to the people affected. He looked more closely at the picture. A metal cross lay among the rubble.

"Moira, look at this."

"Oh, yes, the earthquake in Sicily. It looks like a collapsed church," she said.

"I might have just had a great idea…" he said.

Father John explained his plan to the bishop later that day.

"It's a madcap idea," the bishop said.

Father pulled out his phone and showed the bishop examples of buildings which had been taken down in one place and rebuilt, brick by brick, in other locations.

"It must cost a fortune," the bishop pointed out.

"There might be a way around it, if we are prepared to be generous."

***

The developer agreed to buy the land for a peppercorn in exchange for relocating Saint Anne's church to the Sicilian town struck by the earthquake. It was a huge job, but the builder would end up with cleared land where they could build homes. They wouldn't have to repurpose the church anymore.

So Saint Anne's church building was taken down, stone by stone, and each piece was marked and catalogued to be shipped to Sicily.

At the other end, the gift prompted a generosity race. The best architects offered their services pro bono and the most skilled engineers ensured the building would withstand another earthquake. Masons, carpenters, electricians, plumbers, conservation experts and parishioners made themselves available to work on the church for free. Even a local botanist got involved—by studying the lichens and mosses on the stonework, she could confirm the correct orientation of each stone. Everyone worked round the clock to ensure the church would be ready for Christmas.

***

On Christmas Eve, as Father John emerged from Catania airport's arrivals, he was instantly pulled into a bear hug by his Sicilian counterpart.

"*Grazie di cuore*—thank you from the bottom of our hearts!" Padre Giorgio exclaimed with shiny eyes.

Moira, Julia, Paul and the other parishioners of Saint Anne were welcomed as warmly. They were hosted in the homes of the Santa Maria parishioners.

The Christmas Mass was celebrated together by Father John and Padre Giorgio in the rebuilt church of Saint Anne and Santa Maria.

During his homily, Padre Giorgio told the story of when he received Father John's email with the unusual offer.

"I thought it was a prank and deleted it. Thankfully, Father John wrote again. Now that your beautiful church lives here, you must come and visit us often. This will always be your parish too."

6. A SEASON FOR LOVE

Sofia checked her Christmas shopping list one last time before going back to the car.

A sewing box for Piero, tick. The knitting machine for Irene, tick. Cookie cutters for Andrea, tick. The painting kit for Chiara and the playdough for Irene. Thank goodness the doll that Luca had seen in the window was still there!

When the shopkeeper told her she was buying the last one, Sofia gave such a sigh of relief that other customers turned to look.

Christmas shopping had always been stressful, but now that she was on her own and the number of grandchildren had grown, it was getting harder.

When Carlo was alive, he would help her plan the trip, prioritise shops to visit, and help carry the bags.

But, most importantly, he would spot the signs of her patience fraying and promptly suggest a visit to a café in good time.

She pressed the car's remote key, opened the boot and put her bags in.

Ah, what a relief!

She massaged the crooks of her elbows and wrists where the bags' handles had cut in.

"Excuse me?" a man's voice said behind her.

Sofia turned around. A gentleman with a crop of greying hair and sparky sky-blue eyes was looking at her with a cocked eyebrow and a car key in his hand.

"Yes?" she responded.

"I'm always happy to receive presents," he said, "but are you sure that you want to give me all that?"

"I beg your pardon?"

He pointed the key to the car and pressed it. The car flashed its orange lights and beeped.

"Oh, I must have dropped my key, thank you!" Sofia cried.

She stretched out her hand but he didn't give her the key.

"I think that you'll find that this isn't your car," he said with an amused smile.

"What?" She looked around.

An identical car was parked three spaces down. She rummaged in her handbag, whipped out the key and pressed it. The car responded with flashing lights and a beep. Her car!

The gentleman was right: she had indeed loaded her shopping into his boot and asked him to hand her his key!

Heat rose to her cheeks.

"I'm really sorry. Our cars are identical, and I find Christmas shopping a little stressful," she said.

The man smiled kindly.

"You have nothing to apologise for," he said. "You couldn't have got into the wrong car if I hadn't forgotten to lock it. And, as you can see, you're not the only one who finds Christmas shopping a little stressful. My wife used to do it for us but I'm on my own now. At least you've been successful." He gestured to the bags she had loaded into his car boot, and Sofia felt her cheeks heat up again. "Instead, I've run out of the shops empty-handed," he continued. He opened his empty arms and they laughed.

"I'm Teodoro," he introduced himself.

"Nice to meet you. I'm Sofia," she said in turn.

"What was on your shopping list that you didn't manage to buy?"

He scratched the back of his head and looked sheepishly at his feet.

"Actually, I haven't written down a list…" he admitted. "That's probably the first of my

51

problems. The second is that I have no idea about what some of the things my grandchildren asked for are. For example, is a French knitting doll a doll with knitting needles, or is it a doll which speaks French?"

Sofia smiled. She had used French knitting dolls all her life and they weren't dolls at all.

"Give me a moment to put away my shopping—in my car this time," she said, "and I'll show you where you can buy one."

***

"I think this is all," he said, staring in disbelief at the shopping bags full of presents he carried.

This beautiful stranger had helped him wade through the Christmas shopping, and he was now safely out the other side.

"I don't know how to thank you for all your help," he said. "Can I offer you a cup of coffee?"

She hesitated.

Oh no, he had been too forward. Sofia had helped him out of kindness and now he was making her uncomfortable. She probably had a husband waiting for her.

"I'm sorry, I shouldn't have presumed..." he mumbled.

"I'd love a cup of coffee," she hurried to say.

Something in his heart flipped, a mixture of

excitement and panic. Was there something nearby? He looked around.

"There's a café round the corner." She smiled.

The place was cosy and cheerful, with display fridges full of ice cream and desserts.

"This is my favourite place. The owners make everything themselves," she said, pointing to the content of the fridges.

Teodoro nodded distractedly. The dainty table between them was too small for a man with legs like a cricket to sit opposite a woman he had just met, and he was concentrating hard on not bumping knees with her.

"Do you come here often?" he asked.

A shadow flitted across her face.

"My husband used to take me here when he was alive," she said.

***

Sofia hadn't felt so at ease with a stranger since… she couldn't remember when.

They talked about their lives, their families and all the Christmas preparations they had to do, as though they were old friends catching up, not strangers who met in a car park.

They blissfully sat at their table, heedless of the passing time, and eventually a waitress came over with the bill.

The prospect of saying goodbye to Teodoro

and never seeing him again was like icy water on warm skin.

"You said your Christmas tree is still up in your loft," Teodoro began. "I was thinking…"—he looked into his clasped hands—"…maybe… if you want, I could help you take it down…"

Was it just the heat of the little room that made his cheeks suddenly flush?

"I'd love you to come over and help me," Sofia murmured, and her cheeks felt very hot too.

***

The lasagna was in the oven, the tree was up and all the presents were sitting nicely under its tinselled branches.

Teodoro had helped her with everything, and she had helped him right back. They had seen each other every day. When one of them panicked about *pandoro* being sold out, the other suggested a shop which might have some. When one of them ran out of wrapping paper, the other brought some over.

With Teodoro by her side, preparing for the festivities had been a breeze.

But now, even though her whole family was with her, she felt a little lonely, just because he wasn't there.

If only… no, what a silly thought! Of course

he should spend the day with his family. Christmas was for family, not for friends. But a corner of her heart wished he could be more than a friend…

"Did you take the tree down from the loft on your own?" her eldest daughter, Vania, asked suspiciously.

"I didn't. I had help," Sofia replied awkwardly, busying herself with the salad.

Teodoro filled her heart with so much happiness, but her brain kept asking the difficult questions. How would her family react to her having a close male friend? What if they disapproved?

She didn't want to mar the happiness of Christmas, so she kept her mouth closed and cut up the salad.

The meal went beautifully and everyone loved their presents.

"Can you see the angel at the top of the tree? Teodoro put it up for me!" she almost said, in a reckless moment.

But she stopped herself. An announcement like that would be followed by questions that she wouldn't know how to answer. It would be madness to ruin a good Christmas.

"This is for you, Grandma," Piero told her, putting a parcel on her lap.

It had come in the post, but not straight

from a shop, and the address was handwritten.

"Why did you send it through the post if you knew you were coming, sweetheart?" she asked.

"It's not from me, Nonna."

"Oh. Who is it from, then?" Sofia said, glancing around, but her daughters shook their heads.

"Open it, Nonna!" the children shouted excitedly.

Suddenly her fingers started to tremble. Could it be from…Teodoro?

No, it couldn't be. He hated shopping and had needed her help to buy the presents for his grandchildren! She hadn't got him anything and she had no reason to expect that he should.

Still, as all her family watched her unpeeling the brown tape in total silence, her hands went clammy.

The parcel inside was tied with a velvet ribbon that ended in a wonky bow. Just the way Teodoro would tie a bow.

Her heart hammered inside her chest. She couldn't wait any longer and tore the wrapping paper. A beautiful fascinator lay inside a box.

"Wow, Mum! Who sends you presents like that? Read the card!" her daughters ordered.

A little envelope had dropped to the floor. Sofia picked it up and opened it very slowly, while her blood rushed through her ears like a torrent.

It was an invitation to a New Year's black tie dinner party. From Teodoro.

Her heart flipped and her checks burned.

"Who is it from?" the children demanded.

"It's from a new friend of mine," she murmured. "His name is Teodoro. He's inviting me to a New Year's party."

She lifted her gaze to check her daughters' reaction, but instead of disapproval on their faces she saw surprise. For a beat, silence hung over the room.

"Did you know that Teodoro means 'gift from God'?" Vania said. "I think that's just the right name for him."

Her other daughters nodded and Sofia's heart soared with relief.

***

The fascinator suited her to a tee. It was a miracle it did, because when the shopkeeper had asked him for a description of the lady he was buying it for, all he had told her was that she was beautiful.

All through the dinner, Teodoro couldn't help looking at Sofia. Indeed, she didn't need any fascinator. She was fascinating enough on her own merits, he thought, and tonight she was even more beautiful.

He had no idea if it was the wine or her presence, but he was drunk with happiness.

When it was time for the New Year countdown, they picked up their glasses and stood closer together than they ever had before.

"Three…two…one…Happy New Year!" the dinner host shouted into the microphone.

People cheered, bottles were uncorked and party horns hooted. But when Teodoro turned to Sofia to wish her happy New Year, he was lost in the depths of her eyes.

He was so lost that he bent down and kissed her, and she kissed him back.

"Happy New Year, Sofia. I hope to spend many more with you," he said, his voice breaking.

"I hope that too," she replied with a warm smile.

7. A GIFT THAT KEEPS ON GIVING

Daria instantly recognised her husband's grin.

"Open it," Renato prompted, handing her a parcel wrapped in pink paper.

"Didn't we agree that we weren't doing anniversary presents?" she reproached him, secretly pleased.

"It's only a small thing."

The "small" thing was a box weighing as much as a bottle of Prosecco.

"You didn't have to," Daria protested as she removed the wrapping.

Under the paper was a cardboard box with beautiful orchid prints. Could it contain a scarf with that pattern? Or a silky dressing gown?

Daria smiled in expectation, but when she lifted the lid, her smile faltered. Inside the box was a large bottle of bubble bath.

"You really didn't have to." This time she meant it.

Renato grinned. "My pleasure, darling."

***

Daria opened her bathroom cabinet and placed the bubble bath on the shelf next to the others. She'd received lavender, rose, honeysuckle and Parma violet, and now she had a vanilla-scented one too.

What was she going to do with all those bottles?

One day, when the children were grown up, she might have time for luxuries like bubble baths.

An idea flashed across her mind. Her sister had just got engaged. If Daria put the bottle back in its box and wrapped it again, it would make a lovely present.

***

"Thank you for making time for a cup of coffee with me," Amanda said to her older sister.

Daria was so busy with work and family Amanda hadn't seen her for a while.

"A coffee was long overdue." Daria pulled out of her shopping bag a beautifully wrapped parcel. "Plus, I wanted to celebrate your engagement properly."

"Oh, thank you!"

Amanda had been a little disappointed by her family's reaction to the news of her engagement. Because she and John had been living together for a while, their engagement had been taken for granted by their families. It was so nice that her sister was bothering to celebrate it with her.

She unwrapped the parcel, but when she read the French writing on the box, *bain moussant*, her excitement dropped. Bubble bath—one of the things the doctor had told her to avoid because of her eczema.

Amanda kept smiling. "Thank you, Daria." It was still thoughtful of her sister to give her an engagement present. "How lovely!"

Daria beamed. "I knew you'd like it. Tell me all about your plans!"

Amanda put her disappointment aside. Her sister had got her an engagement present, had made time for her and was interested in her wedding. As for the bubble bath, she already knew someone else who would enjoy it.

***

"You never forget my birthday!" Giovanna exclaimed, taking the present her youngest sister, Amanda, was offering her.

"How could I forget? Mum always made chocolate cake on your birthday," Amanda pointed out.

"Those were the days. I could eat chocolate cake without putting on weight!" Giovanna reminisced.

"Open your present," Amanda told her, grinning with anticipation.

Giovanna removed the wrapping paper and was pleased to read the name of a skincare company.

But when she opened the box, a waft of vanilla hit her nostrils. Instantly, she was hungry. It was like walking into a candy shop. A vanilla-scented bubble bath! It was already giving her sugar cravings with the bottle closed.

"Thank you," she said to her sister, then quickly put the bottle back into the box and closed the lid.

"I knew you'd like a vanilla bubble bath," Amanda said, looking pleased with herself.

"Yes, I love it," Giovanna fibbed.

It was kind of Amanda to remember her birthday. That was what mattered.

Once Amanda had gone, Giovanna rewrapped the box and left the house.

She knew exactly who would love this gift.

***

Beniamino opened the door of his flat to his first visitor.

"Congratulations on your new home!" his sister Giovanna said, handing him a beautifully wrapped box. "I won't be able to come to your house-warming, so I thought I'd give you something to enjoy in your new home."

"Thank you!" Beniamino replied, hugging her. "Are you staying for a tour?"

"I can't right now," Giovanna told him. "Another time."

He put the box down on the kitchen counter and started unwrapping it.

How sweet of his sister to pop round and bring him a present! Judging by the smell, it was something delicious to eat.

Beniamino finally lifted the lid of the box to see it contained bubble bath. He didn't have a bathtub. Oh, well, it was the thought that counted, and Giovanna couldn't have known.

He stashed the box at the back of a cupboard and promptly forgot about it. All he remembered was that Giovanna had been nice to him about his new home.

**

"I don't know how I'm going to get through Christmas. After buying the flat, I'm skint," Beniamino confided to a colleague, Elio, at lunch the next day. "I haven't started my Christmas shopping yet, and I have no money."

"Do you have anything to regift?" Elio suggested.

"But I can't flog unwanted gifts off on someone else," Beniamino replied.

"Regifting doesn't mean that you don't

appreciate the gifts you received, or that you don't care about the people who gave them," his friend pointed out.

Beniamino considered this. "Maybe it's not such a bad idea," he admitted.

"Just make sure you don't give something back to the person who gave it to you."

As soon as Beniamino got home, he searched his flat. He found plenty of things he had never used and was unlikely to use in the future. For each of them, he could think of a perfect recipient.

***

It was Christmas Day and Beniamino and his siblings were gathered at their parents' house to celebrate and exchange presents. So far, Ben's regifting had gone well and everyone had enjoyed his presents.

His niece picked up Beniamino's fabric-wrapped parcel and brought it to her granny.

"This is for you from Beniamino," she announced.

"Such lovely wrapping!" Beniamino's mum exclaimed, untying the knots. "How nice—a bottle of vanilla bubble bath!" She lifted the bottle for everyone to see.

Silence fell on the room.

Renato glanced at Daria, who looked at Amanda, who turned to Giovanna, who looked at Beniamino.

Suddenly remembering that the bottle had been Giovanna's gift to him, Beniamino realised he had messed up!

As soon as the presents were all opened, everyone got up to prepare the table for the Christmas lunch. Beniamino looked for Giovanna. He had to explain to her that he had given her present away because he didn't have a bathtub.

But when he found her, she was talking to Amanda.

"I'm so sorry," Giovanna was telling her sister, "but your bubble bath smelled so delicious that it gave me sugar cravings."

So the bubble bath had been a present to her from Amanda!

"No need to apologise," Amanda replied. "I did the same thing. I received the bottle from Daria as an engagement present. I thought it was lovely, but bubble baths are a no-no for my eczema."

Beniamino overheard Renato speaking to Daria.

"That's the same type of bubble bath I gave you. It must be very popular!"

As he joined the dots, Beniamino smiled to himself. The bubble bath Renato had given Daria was the one Daria had given Amanda.

They'd all regifted the bottle until it had reached the person who would enjoy it: their mum.

He still needed to clarify things with Giovanna.

When he was finally alone with her, she prevented his apology.

"Don't worry about it," Giovanna assured him. "I'm only curious to know why you didn't keep it. Did it make you hungry too?"

Beniamino laughed. "I don't have a bathtub!"

"I should have taken up your offer of a tour!" Giovanna replied with a grin.

***

"It was very nice of your mum and dad to give us a weekend break as a Christmas present," Renato said to Daria when they got home.

"Yes," his wife agreed. "It'll be very nice to have a bit of time with just the two of us while they babysit."

"Maybe you'll finally get to have a bubble bath," Renato remarked.

Daria smiled. "I am looking forward to it," she replied, pulling Renato towards her for a kiss.

8. THE WHOLE PACKAGE

Every Christmas, Olivia, Lavinia, Giulia and Ania met at their favourite café to pull out of a hat who would be Secret Santa for whom.

"I have an idea," Olivia announced. "This year we won't write down just our names, but also what we'd like to receive."

The owner of the café arrived with their orders.

He put the macchiato in front of Ania and asked who had ordered the cappuccino, the espresso and the hot chocolate. When he had gone, they resumed their conversation.

"I think Olivia's idea is good. It'll save us the mental load of choosing what to buy," Lavinia stated.

"The gift doesn't necessarily have to be purchased," Giulia added.

"Yes, and our usual price limit still applies," Olivia reminded everyone.

They all got pieces of paper and thought

about what they might like to receive from their Secret Santa.

***

The others had already dropped their pieces of paper into the hat, but Ania had no idea what to write.

She would have found it a lot easier to think of presents for them rather than for herself. She didn't care about material stuff. There was only one thing she wished with all her heart, but her friends couldn't give it to her: a boyfriend. She had tried online dating without success.

"Ania can't decide between all the things she wants," Giulia joked. "Choose whatever came to your mind first."

To get it over and done with, Ania covered her paper with her hand, scribbled *A boyfriend*, and dropped it into the hat.

Whoever got to be her Secret Santa would realise it was a joke and give her something else.

***

Giulia stared at the paper. How could she give Ania a boyfriend? Not even the real Santa could procure such a present.

But she wasn't going to give away her dismay because the first rule of a Secret Santa was secrecy.

She smiled, refolded the paper and dropped it into her pocket.

She continued drinking her coffee, eating her cake and chatting with the others, but all the while she thought about Ania's request.

Should she create an online dating profile on Ania's behalf?

No. Posing as Ania felt wrong.

Maybe she could organise a blind date.

No. She had been on some and never enjoyed them.

Giulia decided that Ania's gift request was too big for her on her own. She was going to ask Olivia and Lavinia for help.

So Giulia, Lavinia and Olivia met at their usual café the following afternoon. They ordered their usual drinks and, as usual, were served by the owner who couldn't remember what each one had ordered.

"You could organise a dinner party with eligible bachelors," Lavinia suggested once Giulia had told them the problem.

"I don't know any eligible bachelors," Giulia admitted.

"Doesn't Matteo have single friends?"

"Most of our friends are couples."

"How about colleagues?"

"Most of his colleagues are men. There must be some single ones among them," Giulia reflected.

So they organised a Christmas dinner party.

***

Ania was suspicious about this invitation. Giulia had never thrown a party for her friends and Matteo's colleagues together. The two groups didn't have anything in common.

One explanation could be that Giulia was Ania's Secret Santa and had taken her gift request seriously.

Ania had regretted it as soon as she'd dropped the paper into the hat. But it was too late now. She couldn't disappoint Giulia by not turning up to the dinner party she was organising for her. So Ania got ready and was about to leave her house when she looked outside.

Snow covered her car, her drive and the road, and it was still falling fast. It would be too dangerous to drive to Giulia's in the next village. Ania picked up the phone and called her friend to cancel.

***

After the dinner party failure, Giulia, Olivia and Lavinia called another meeting without Ania.

As they trudged into the café with heavy hearts, even the café's owner looked disappointed. They ordered their usual drinks and, as usual, the man couldn't remember who had ordered what. The three friends found that routine comforting.

"We need a new plan," Lavinia said. "Ania never told me, but I'm sure she used to have a crush on my brother. He's single now and I think that he and Ania would get on very well."

"And you'd love to have Ania as your sister-in-law," Olivia pointed out.

Lavinia looked sheepish. "Well, there's that too."

"If we organise another dinner party, Ania will get suspicious," Giulia reasoned.

"We won't. Lavinia will organise a chance meeting at her place," Olivia said.

Everyone agreed that it was a good plan.

***

"It's so nice to live close to each other," Ania told Lavinia as they shared a pot of coffee.

Lavinia had called Ania over with the pretext of asking her opinion on some new curtains.

"Absolutely," Lavinia agreed, cradling her cup.

There was more coffee in the pot for her brother, who should arrive any moment. She'd called him over with the excuse of giving him a parcel for their parents, as she'd heard he planned on visiting them next weekend.

"I love our village. It's like a family. I

couldn't live in a big city where everyone is a stranger," Ania continued.

"Me neither," Lavinia replied.

The doorbell rang then and Lavinia rushed to open it.

"Ania is here too," she told her brother. "We're having coffee. Will you join us?"

Giacomo agreed eagerly.

When she saw him, Ania greeted him warmly. "I haven't seen you in a long time. How are you?"

They chatted for a bit, then Giacomo turned to Lavinia.

"When you called me, I was planning to come to see you anyway. I have some news," he told her with a smile.

A shiver ran down Lavinia's back. Please, let it not be a new girlfriend!

"I've been offered a promotion," he told her.

Relief flooded Lavinia.

"There's just one thing." He looked sheepishly into his cup. "The job's in Japan."

Oh, no. Her matchmaking plan was off. Ania would never leave the village, let alone the country.

"I'll come back for all the holidays and I'll have a spare room for you to visit whenever you want," Giacomo added, misinterpreting

Lavinia's disappointed expression.

***

The boyfriend project task force met again at the café.

"As you two have failed, I'm stepping in," Olivia announced.

Olivia's plan was big: a reunion for their school year.

"That's potentially two hundred people," Lavinia pointed out.

"There's not enough time before Christmas," Giulia added. "We won't find a venue at such short notice."

But Olivia was confident that she could pull it off.

She contacted their old school and arranged to rent the gym for the first night of the school's Christmas holidays. A friend of hers would provide the catering and another one the entertainment. Through word of mouth and social media she reached all the people in their school year that wanted to be reached. Including a very special someone…

Back at school, Ania had liked Alberto a lot. His social media profile stated that he was single.

"If Ania doesn't like him anymore, there will be other single men at the party," Olivia reasoned.

***

When Ania heard that Olivia was organising a school reunion, she had no doubt it was for her benefit.

Her friends' matchmaking efforts were getting out of control. And they were putting her under pressure because, if she didn't meet a suitable match at this party, they'd be disappointed.

Olivia had let slip that Alberto was coming. Maybe there was hope, Ania thought.

On the day of the event, Ania discovered that time had made Alberto even more handsome than she remembered him.

The insecurity of youth had given way to an attractive confidence. He seemed as pleased to see her as she was to see him. As they caught up with each other, Ania wondered if he could be her Secret Santa's wish come true.

But as the evening went on, some things about Alberto jarred with her.

He seemed to pay attention only to attractive single women while he ignored everyone else. He was a good dancer, but he didn't seem to worry about taking up other people's space. At one point, he made an unkind comment about how one of their classmates had aged.

Despite these things, when he asked her if

she'd like to go somewhere else for a drink, Ania was tempted to give him a chance.

She was about to say yes when someone knocked his elbow, causing him to spill his drink on the floor.

"Sorry," the guy said nervously.

"Clumsy idiot," Alberto snapped at the man, who looked mortified and moved away.

Alberto turned to Ania. "He's a loser. At school, he used to burst into tears when we teased him."

Ania was horrified. No matter how good a dancer, how debonair his conversation, how suave his manners, Ania would not go out with this bully.

***

The day the friends had set for exchanging their Secret Santa gifts arrived.

Ania entered the café with trepidation. She wouldn't put it past her friends to turn up at the café with a random bachelor from the street wrapped in wrapping paper and tinsel.

Thankfully, she found only Giulia, Olivia and Lavinia at their usual table with no suspiciously large parcels.

"I'm sorry, Ania. I've been unable to source your present," Giulia apologised.

"Don't be," Ania replied, looking at her feet. "It was unfair of me to ask for something that

I should have looked for by myself."

"I've got you something else." Giulia extracted a parcel from her handbag. "A consolation prize."

Ania felt tears prick her eyes.

"You didn't have to get me another present. You three have already given me the best present ever."

Giulia, Lavinia and Olivia looked at each other in confusion.

"Your friendship. I've seen how hard you have worked for me. I couldn't have asked for better friends."

They all hugged across the table.

The café's owner, who was on his way with the tray of their orders, stopped at a respectful distance. When they'd finished hugging, he came over with a smile.

"Your macchiato," he said, putting down Ania's order in front of her.

Then he held out the cappuccino until Giulia claimed it, and did the same for the other two drinks.

When he was out of earshot, Giulia narrowed her eyes.

"Have you noticed how he never remembers our orders except for Ania's?" she whispered.

Smiles spread across their faces. "He likes

you, Ania."

Ania glanced at the counter and met the man's eyes. He smiled at her.

Ania opened her present from Giulia. It was a beautiful coffee gift set.

"Thank you!"

"But promise that you won't stop getting your coffee here," Giulia replied.

"Definitely not. In fact, I have a feeling I might be coming here more often from now on," Ania said with a wink.

Whether her Secret Santa wish would come true soon or not, she had her three friends who had shown that they loved her very much. And this was more than she could ever have hoped for.

9. SNOW PROBLEMS

Melina sighed as the hero and heroine kissed under the mistletoe, surrounded by glittering snow and fir trees.

"Nonna, why do they have snow at Christmas in the movies, but we never do?" her granddaughter, Valentina, asked.

"Palermo is too far south, but every now and then we've had some snow too. I'll show you." Melina pulled one of her photo albums from the bookshelf. "This photo was taken in the winter of 1981. Look how much snow we got. It was almost too deep for your mother's rubber boots. Here are some photos of me and your grandfather when we were just engaged."

Melina still remembered fondly that trip to the Madonie mountains, in the Sicilian hinterland.

Valentina's eyes widened. "You and Nonno can ski?"

"Not really. We had a day's lesson, just to

try."

"I can't imagine Nonno doing that," Valentina said categorically.

Neither could Melina. These days Tanino was so averse to novelty, change and any kind of risk that she could hardly reconcile the man of today with the one in the photo.

He had never been a daredevil, but he had been adventurous enough to capture her interest among all the other young men in their neighbourhood.

Melina turned the page. "Here is your mamma in the snow again." A five-year-old Giovanna was grinning on the balcony of their flat, pretending to lick the snow. "She said that it was ice cream from heaven."

Valentina studied the photo. "Mamma looks younger than me and I've not seen snow yet," she moaned.

"I'm sorry, darling. It just hasn't snowed here in the last few years."

"What about the mountains where you and Nonno tried skiing?"

"There should be snow there now…Maybe we could take you there. Let's talk to your nonno."

***

Tanino was dozing in front of the kitchen TV. The football match was over, and they were showing a nature programme on the sloths of the American rainforests.

Melina and Valentina walked in and Tanino immediately sensed that they were looking for him. He stiffened.

Valentina stood between him and the TV. "Nonno, will you take me to see the snow?"

"There's no snow here, darling."

"That's why I want you to take me to the mountains."

Tanino darted a glance at Melina. She must be behind this crazy idea.

She shrugged and opened her arms.

"Please, Nonno. I've never seen snow," Valentina pleaded.

Tanino tried to remember the last time he had been to the Madonie mountains. It was probably when he and Melina were newly engaged. He remembered that day trip very well.

It had been hard going reaching the skiing station, and he hadn't enjoyed the cold snow sneaking into the cracks between his clothes and melting onto his skin. In fifty years of marriage he had managed to avoid going back. Had his luck run out now?

"We need chains for the car tyres, and I don't have any."

"We don't need to go all the way to the top.

You can drive us to the beginning of the snow, stop in a layby, then go home."

Tanino glanced at the sleeping sloth on the TV screen and couldn't help envying him.

***

The road was busier than Tanino had expected. Maybe going on New Year's Eve hadn't been a such a good idea.

After a few hairpin bends, the first Swiss-style chalets appeared on the flanks of the mountains, and splatters of snow dotted the slopes and the road verges.

"Snow!" Valentina cried, bouncing in her seat.

"Stop here and we'll be happy," Melina told him.

"I can't. There's no layby and I have cars behind."

"Just go a little further," Melina suggested.

"The road sign says not to proceed without chains."

"We're only going a little further."

Snowflakes had started to splatter against the windscreen.

"What's that?" Valentina asked.

"It's snowing!" Melina announced.

Valentina squealed.

"Be quiet! I need to concentrate," Tanino begged.

The car in front had slowed down and a queue of traffic had formed. Tanino noticed that his car was the only one without snow chains. What if they got stuck?

He was desperate to turn around and drive home, but there was nowhere to turn around or stop. He should never have agreed to this crazy idea.

After the next bend, the mountain refuge and resort appeared. There was bound to be somewhere to turn around there. How he longed for his chair by the TV!

When they got to the car park, the snow was so deep that the car was skidding all over the place. Tanino managed to slide gently into a parking space.

"There's no way we can drive down without chains," he said with a sigh.

"Look at the snowflakes!" Valentina pointed.

"We'll have to spend the night here," Melina reasoned.

"The car park is full. The resort must be fully booked up for the New Year's party," Tanino said.

"Yes, but this isn't just a resort. It's a mountain refuge, and refuges aren't allowed to turn people away," Melina explained.

She had seen it in a documentary about

mountain climbers in the Alps.

They walked into reception and explained the situation. The receptionist confirmed that all the tourist rooms were booked, but that they would be given food and shelter in the alpine refuge section of the resort.

"How much will it cost?" Tanino asked, glancing at the fancy wood panelling and animal trophies on the walls.

"A donation."

That answer wiped the frown from Tanino's face.

Melina rang Valentina's parents to tell them what had happened, and they promised they would try to reach them the following day with an extra set of snow chains. For that night— New Year's Eve—they were going to have to weather it out there.

"Aren't we having an adventure!" Melina exclaimed.

Valentina grinned. Tanino groaned.

***

Their room turned out to be a spartan-looking dormitory lined with rows of metal-framed bunk beds. The blankets felt like thick cardboard, the sheets like sandpaper, and the musty smell of the room suggested that it was really only used for emergencies.

"Isn't it a luxury to have the entire room for

ourselves," Melina said.

Tanino didn't say anything, but Valentina had climbed to the top bunk.

"I'm the queen of the castle!" she called out.

Melina chose a bottom bunk.

As soon as she felt their pillows, she felt sorry for Tanino. He was used to sleeping with a soft pillow, while these were like bricks. She watched him trying to get himself comfortable on his bed without a word of complaint. Neither did he complain when they were turned away from the dining hall and told that they could only have sandwiches in their room as the restaurant was booked.

When they were served cold sandwiches to eat sitting on their beds, Melina felt a little sorry for herself too.

"I miss your pasta bake," Tanino told her.

Back home she had prepared a pasta bake and escalopes for their New Year's Eve dinner with Valentina's parents. She'd even laid the table with the good crockery and cutlery, ready for when they returned from their trip to the snow.

"I'm sorry I pushed you to take us here when you didn't want to," Melina told Tanino.

"It's okay. When we came here fifty years ago, you said that you wanted to come back and maybe spend the night. Do you remember?"

Now that he mentioned it, she did remember it.

"I should have organised this trip long ago. I'm sorry if this isn't the lodging that you had imagined," he said with a kind smile.

Maybe her husband wasn't as adventurous now as when he was younger, but he had certainly grown in patience and kindness.

The next day Michele and Giovanna turned up with an extra set of chains. It had stopped snowing and the snowplough had cleared the roads.

Before heading home, Valentina made a snowman with her parents while Tanino and Melina admired the view of the ski slopes and reminisced about their first trip.

Michele and Giovanna had booked a table at a farm down in the valley.

"Thank you both for your thoughtfulness," Melina told them warmly.

After enjoying a delicious New Year's lunch, they got home in time for supper.

There they found everything ready for the meal that Melina had prepared for the night before, which was very convenient.

For their dessert, Giovanna produced a parcel from the *pasticceria* downstairs. She unwrapped a beautiful mountain of chocolate sponge topped with swirls of white cream and sprinkled with coconut flakes—just like snow.

"How appropriate!" Melina exclaimed, then looked at Giovanna. "Do you remember calling snow—"

"—'the ice cream from heaven'," Giovanna completed Melina's sentence with a chuckle.

10. DEAR SANTA

Roger is tired of his job, especially at Christmas. He's been a postman for forty years and it's always the same at Christmas. There's an avalanche of parcels, cards and letters, seasonal staff who don't know what they're doing, and old hands like him having to show them what to do instead of getting on with their own jobs.

"What do I do with this, Roger?" one of the seasonals, Julie, asks him as they're sorting an ocean of mail.

She shows him a sheet of paper without an envelope.

"Give it to me," Rogers replies, resigned to dealing with the problem.

It's a child's letter to Santa. Usually, letters for the Write To Santa scheme come in a stamped envelope, addressed to the Royal Mail Santa's address. They also contain the name and address of the sender so that the child can receive a reply.

But this one doesn't have an envelope, a stamp or any address for the sender. A hopeful child must have posted it without their parents' knowledge or help. It's a hopeless case, but Roger doesn't want to throw it away.

Just in case he can find any clue in the letter, Roger reads it.

***

Dear Santa. It's me, Ilaria. I know it's a little early to tell you what I'd like for Christmas, but I want to ask you for something big so I'm giving you time to organise it.

If you can't give me the gift I want, please tell me and I will ask the Befana. You are my first choice because the Befana brings gifts to children in Italy and I live in England. I'm only half-Italian so I don't know if she would bring a present to me too. Also, the Befana brings gifts on January the 6th and I don't want to wait that long.

I want you to bring my mummy home for Christmas. She's in Italy, I think. It's a long way, but you've got a flying sleigh so it should be easy for you.

Daddy says that she's gone because she doesn't like living in England. But don't worry: I'm sure that, when she sees your sleigh, she will want to come with you. Who wouldn't want a ride on your sleigh? I do.

In fact, if she doesn't want to come with you, you could take me to her instead. That would be fun.

But I'd prefer if you bring her here because I want to spend Christmas with Daddy and Mummy, the three of us together. Please.

Love, Ilaria

PS. I've just thought something. If Mummy wants to spend Christmas with her mummy and her daddy, Nonna and Nonno, then maybe you could bring them too?

If there's not enough space on your sleigh, Mummy and Nonna and Nonno can put the bag of gifts on their laps. It's okay; they won't mind. Sometimes I do that when I go with Dad on the tractor. Thank you!

***

Roger feels a hard lump in his chest. He remembers when his mother left him and his father.

Back then, it was very shameful for a woman to leave her husband. Leaving a child was inconceivable. All through his life, Roger has carried the guilt and shame of what his mother did.

As a child, he was convinced that he must have been very bad if his mothcr had done what no other mother would. Growing up, he told himself that she might have had her own issues—nothing to do with him.

But deep inside Roger, the small child who felt responsible and guilty never left him, and he's still there.

So now Roger's eyes are moist for this little girl, and for himself, and he wishes with all his heart that he could deliver this letter to the one person who could make the girl's wish come true. But how, without an address?

Still, he can't throw this letter away. He folds it and stuffs it in his shirt pocket.

"So what do we do with letters like this?" Julie asks him, looking confused.

"We keep them close to our heart," he says, and goes back to the sorting belt.

***

Dear Santa. It's me again, Ilaria. I haven't heard back from you, so I guess that you'll bring me my mummy and I don't have to ask the Befana. Thank you!

Unfortunately there's a little problem. Today Uncle Tom came to get some hay from Daddy. "Why has Alessia left you?" he asked Daddy.

"She needed to find herself," Daddy said.

So Mummy has got lost!

Please, could you find her? If she's got lost here, you could look in the woods around Daddy's farm. If she's got lost in Italy, you could look near Nonna and Nonno's shop.

It's the shop with the red door and all the books in the window, in front of the big fountain where tourists throw coins in the water. Please find her quickly! Thank you so much!

Love, Ilaria.

***

Roger's heart skips a beat. He recognised the handwriting at once and now he recognises the name too.

Again there's no envelope and no address. Just *To Santa* scribbled on the top of the folded sheet.

But now there are some clues.

There must be many fountains in Italy, but if this one is a favourite with tourists, maybe he could find out where it is, find the shop of the girl's grandparents and send the two letters there.

"I've been to Italy a few times," Julie says, looking over Roger's shoulders.

Rogers doesn't know how, but wherever he turns she's always around him. A few days ago, she asked him if he was single and suggested they had lunch together! What a cheek! Hasn't anybody told her that he doesn't do those sorts of things?

It's not that he doesn't like Julie. She's a lovely-looking woman the same age as him. And she's been through a lot, losing her husband and bringing up her children all on her own—she's already told him her life story.

Roger likes her a lot, but he doesn't do romance and relationships. If marriage didn't work out for his father, why should it work out for him? Why should he be good enough for a wife if he wasn't good enough even for his own mother?

So Roger keeps declining Julie's approaches and waits for her to leave when the Christmas rush is over.

"Do you know where this fountain is?" Roger asks her.

"I'm not sure, but I think we can find out if we go online and search. How about we go to the café after our shifts? It's not a date, don't worry," she says with a smile.

Roger's first instinct is to say no. He's never been with a woman to a café—or anywhere else. But Julie has reassured him that it's not a date, and he's desperate to help the child.

"Okay," he agrees.

***

Julie is already sitting at a table when Roger arrives.

His hands are clammy and he reminds himself that this is not a date. It's just about the fountain and the girl who needs his help.

His whole body is shaking and, when he tries to sit in front of Julie without brushing her knees, he knocks the table. The holly and pine centrepiece topples from the table onto Julie's lap.

Roger feels his cheeks colour with embarrassment, and he eyes the door, imaging he could run away. But the little girl needs him and Julie can help him. He must stay.

"What would you like?" he asks her, so that he can at least escape to the counter.

"A cup of tea and a slice of Christmas cake, please," she replies.

He studies the drinks menu on the wall, taking deep breaths. Then he orders two cups of tea and a slice of Christmas cake.

"Nothing to eat for you?" Julie asks him when he returns with the drinks and only one plate of cake.

"I'm not hungry," he tells her, which is perfectly true. He lost his appetite the moment he agreed to this meeting.

"Then we'll share this cake. It's too much for me," she says, pushing the cake into the middle and handing him a fork from the jar on the table.

He's never shared a dish with anyone.

"No, thanks," he says, but she still gives him the fork.

Then she shows him her phone, where she's already searched for famous Italian fountains and has come up with a shortlist. Now they add the word "coins" to their search and one fountain comes at the top of the results.

"The Trevi Fountain in Rome, of course!"
Julie exclaims. "The legend goes that, if you
toss a coin in the Trevi Fountain, you will
return to Rome. If you toss two, you will also
find love. With tree coins, you'll get married."

Roger avoids her gaze.

Then they use Google's street-view map and
check out the square where the fountain sits.
Yes, there's a bookshop with a red door! They
find the bookshop's full address with postcode.

Roger pulls out of his pocket the envelope
and stamp he's bought for this purpose, and
addresses it. Then he puts the child's letters
inside.

"Hopefully they'll reach the mother," he
says.

Julie looks at him with kind, warm eyes.

"You care a lot about other people," she
remarks.

"I know what it's like to spend Christmas
without a mum. I've spent many," he tells Julie.

He doesn't usually tell people about his
childhood, but Julie is starting to grow on him.

"I'm sorry. Did your mother pass away?"

"No. She left us."

Roger doesn't like to say that. He imagines
people thinking that he must be totally
unworthy of love if his own mother left him.

But Julie puts her hand on Roger's arm. Her

hand is soft and warm and makes him feel better.

"I know what it's like. My dad left Mum and me."

Roger feels Julie's love through her hand and her kind eyes, and he feels that he loves her too.

"I'm sorry," he says.

"Never think it's your fault," she tells him.

How does Julie know that this is exactly what he feels?

"I always thought it was my fault," she goes on. "Then my late husband showed me that it wasn't."

"How did he do that?" Roger asks.

"He just showed me that I could be loved."

***

Dear Santa. I've got good news. Mummy is not lost anymore.

Today Grandma came to visit us and brought a box of broken biscuits—the ones she gets from her milkman. They're fantastic! There are custard creams, bourbons and digestives!

While I chose, she and Daddy went to the kitchen.

Grown-ups always think that children can't hear, but we can hear very well if we're paying attention, so I heard them talking.

"Has Alessia found someone else?" Grandma asked.

"I think so," Daddy said.

So Mummy is not lost anymore and she's even finding other lost people. I'm so proud of her and I can't wait till you bring her home!

I told Daddy that we should buy Mummy's favourite biscuits for when she comes home. He said she wasn't coming home. I told him that you're bringing her back, but he didn't believe me. Could you please reply to me so I can show Daddy it's true? Thank you.

Love, Ilaria.

***

It's Christmas Day! Santa hasn't brought Mummy home yet. I think he's delivering all the other children's presents first and mine last because it's special.

I rush to the window to see if I can spot Santa's sleigh. There's no sleigh but there's snow instead!

The doorbell rings. I run to the key cabinet; I reach on tiptoe and grab the keys. I unlock the door.

"Mummy!" I squeal, jump and hug her. "I knew Santa would bring you back!"

"My treasure..." Mummy says and she kisses me. Her cheeks are wet.

"What's going on?" Daddy asks.

He's in his pyjamas, his hair is sticking out at funny angles and he's rubbing his eyes.

"Merry Christmas, Ed. I hope you don't

mind me..." Mummy says and gives him an envelope.

He opens it and pulls out some papers.

"My letters to Santa!" I cry out.

I thought parents mustn't see their children's letters to Santa, but it's okay. I can't be cross with Santa after he's brought Mummy back!

"How was the ride on the sleigh?" I ask her when we sit down to open the presents she's brought from Italy.

"Very nice. A little windy." She smiles.

We have a wonderful Christmas lunch together, with Christmas crackers and with Italian panettone.

"Have the people you've found gone home for Christmas too?" I ask Mummy.

"What people?" Mummy asks.

"Daddy said you've found someone," I say.

Mummy looks at Daddy. "I didn't find anyone," she says. "All I found was myself, and now I know that I belong here. But I have an open ticket to return to Italy, if you would like me to go."

"Don't go! Stay!" I cry.

Daddy doesn't say anything. He turns on the TV for me, and he and Mummy go to the kitchen to wash up. But I don't watch the TV. Instead, I take a pencil and a piece of paper and

I write two letters: a thank-you letter for Santa and a request to the Befana.

***

Dear Befana.

Am I allowed to ask for another gift, even if I've already had one from Santa? I hope so. The gift I want is that Mummy stays here. Can you do that for me? Thank you!

Love, Ilaria.

***

Mummy and Daddy take ages to do the washing-up. When they come out of the kitchen, they have red eyes. Washing up the Christmas lunch must be very tiring.

"Can we go out and play in the snow?" I ask them.

They look at each other and say yes.

We dress up warm, with gloves, hats and wellies, and we go to the field by the sheep's barn.

The snow is even whiter than the sheep and we make snowmen and snow angels, then we throw snowballs at each other. Daddy throws a lot of snowballs at Mummy.

It starts snowing again.

"I think many flights will be cancelled," Mummy says, looking up at the sky and then at Daddy. "Do you think I could stay?"

"Is that what you want?" Daddy asks. He

looks very serious.

"I do."

"Soon the snow will melt and there will be mud instead. The clouds will give rain and you will miss home again," Daddy says.

"My home is where you two are," Mummy says, looking into his eyes.

"Then we'll be very happy for you to stay," Daddy says.

I look up at the sky and thank the Befana.

***

Julie has invited Roger to her flat for a cup of tea.

This time there are no reasons or excuses for the meeting other than the pleasure of enjoying each other's company. And Roger has said yes.

As he walks into her flat, self-consciously holding a bunch of flowers, he takes in the scent of her home. It's floral with a hint of baking. It's the smell of Julie.

The curtains are bright, the cushions are cheerful and the carpet is soft and clean. He loves it.

He imagines himself living here with her or her living in his flat, making her mark there, and for the first time in his life he's not terrified.

"I thought we could watch a classic movie with a famous scene shot at the Trevi fountain.

What do you think?" she asks him.

The movie is already on the TV, waiting to be played. It's in black-and-white and it's paused at a scene where a beautiful couple are about to kiss.

Roger understands that, if he says yes, his relationship with Julie will progress, but he's not scared.

"Good idea."

They sit close on the sofa and Roger puts his arm over Julie's shoulders. She feels soft and warm and fits perfectly against him.

Roger didn't know that hugging someone could feel so good. He wishes he had realised sooner. But it's never too late, and he's not going to let any more chances of happiness run through his fingers like sand.

In the movie, the beautiful actress in a black evening dress steps into the Trevi fountain. She's been searching for the male actor, calling his name. Finally he arrives. She's letting the fountain's water run over her face and hair, enjoying it. She calls him in. He's reluctant at first but then he steps in too.

Roger imagines Julie walking into the fountain and calling him in. And it strikes him that, if Julie knew about this movie, she probably already knew, before they met at the café, that the Trevi fountain was the one they were looking for. He smiles to himself at her resourcefulness.

He turns to Julie and she smiles at him.

He's done with being terrified and feeling unworthy. This is Roger's chance to be happy, and he won't let it pass him by.

The End

Other books by Stefania Hartley

In this series:
Sweet Surprises
A Season of Goodwill
Sand, Sea and Tamburello
To Be Loved
Drive Me Crazy
What's Yours is Mine
Stars Are Silver
A Slip of the Tongue
Confetti and Lemon Blossom
Fresh from the Sea

Other collections of short stories:
Good Habits
Welcome to Quayside
Tales from the Parish
Keeping It Cool

Romance novellas:
How to Choose a Husband
The Italian Fake Date
Sweet Competition for Camillo's Café
Second Chances at Mamma's Trattoria
Under Far Eastern Skies

Cosy mysteries:
Father Roberto and the Missing Money
Father Roberto and the Runaway Ring
Father Roberto and the Rural Riots
Father Roberto and the Mystery of the
Microscope

ABOUT THE AUTHOR

Stefania was born in Sicily and immediately started growing, but not very much. She left her sunny island after falling in love with an Englishman, and now she lives in the UK with her husband and their three children.

Having finally learnt English, she's enjoying it so much that she now writes novels and short stories which have been longlisted, shortlisted, commended, and won prizes.

If you have enjoyed these stories, please leave a review. To be the first to hear when she's releasing a new book, sign up for her newsletter and receive an exclusive short story: www.stefaniahartley.com/subscribe